NINA'S HOUSE

MAX'S HOUSE

PETROPOLIS
PET DOORS

For Mother

~S. S. W. and C. S.

Published in the United States in 2004
by Handprint Books
413 Sixth Avenue
Brooklyn, New York 11215
www.handprintbooks.com
First Edition
Designed by E. Friedman
Printed in China
ISBN: 1-59354-001-9
2 4 6 8 10 9 7 5 3 1

PETROPOLIS

Susanne Santoro Whayne

Illustrations by Christopher Santoro

Handprint Books 🖐 Brooklyn, New York

"Hey, Max!" Dad called.
"Here's your new pet door."
"Hmmm," Molly said,
"I liked his old one more."

"Maxie," Mom warned,
"be good while we're gone."
Ted said, "I'll bet he sleeps
the whole day long."

Max sniffed at his door.
"What's this?" he cried.
"What's going on
in my yard outside?

"Do I smell popcorn?
Is that chocolate ice cream?
I know that's cheese pizza!
This can't be a dream!"

Max pushed at the door.
His excitement grew.
The door swung open—
and Max jumped through.

The dog looked around
in a state of shock.
"This isn't my tree . . .
or my yard . . . or my block!"

And something else had changed—
from his head to his toes.
"Good heavens!" Max yelped.
"I'm wearing clothes!"

A fish on a scooter
pulled into view.
"I take it you're Max?
This is for you."

"Oh, gosh," said Max,
wagging his tail
and tearing the flap.
"I never get mail!"

"Here you go!" said the rabbit,
giving Max a list
of the sights in Petropolis
that shouldn't be missed.

"Just a quick question~"
Max started to say.
"There's your bus!" cried the rabbit.
"Have a great day!"

"Well, look who's here,"
Max said as he sat.
"It's my next-door neighbor,
Nina the cat!"

"I often," she told Max,
"come here on my own
to enjoy the city
when my family's not home."

"Nina," Max said,
"this day just got better!
We can enjoy
the city together.

"By the way," he said,
"I've a question for you~"
"Not now," Nina cried,
"there's a movie at two!"

"This is the life,"
Max called from a chair.
"We can lie on the furniture,
and no one will care!"

After the show,
snacks were a must.
Max had four liver pizzas
on thin rawhide crust.

But they still had room
(dessert never hurt)
for kibble sundaes
at the Slurp n' Burp.

In the art museum,
Maxie's mind was churning.

La Bone Moderne
JEAN ARF

Whiskers Mother
JAMES WHISKER

Mousa Lisa
LIZARDO DA VINCI

The Three Cats
PABLO PICATSSO

Sunflowers
VINCENT VAN GOAT

He wasn't so sure
about ever returning.

The Thinker
AUGUSTE RODENT

"I love it here!
I don't want to go back!"
Max was having
a confusion attack!

Number 2
JACKSON the POLLOCK

The Persistence of Kibble
SALVADOR DOGI

Soup Can
ANDY WART HOG

"I know," Nina said,
"I felt the same way.
The first time I came here,
I wanted to stay."

"Before you decide,
take a look at this wall."
Max stared at the painting,
which made him recall . . .

. . . Mom tossing balls,
Dad petting his head,
running with Molly,
naps on Ted's bed.

Dogs Best Friend
NORMAN ROTTWEILER

"You're right!" Max declared.
"I've had a good roam.
So good-bye, dear Nina,
it's time to go home."

He ran down the steps,
then stopped in his tracks.
A huge realization
had just hit Max!

Though he'd tried to ask twice,
he still didn't know . . .
How do I leave here?
Where do I go?

"I'll ask Nina," he cried.
There she was in a taxi.
Too late~she was gone~
waving good-bye to Maxie.

"The rabbit will tell me
which path to take."
The rabbit, however,
had taken a break.

There was no one to help
anywhere in the park,
and when Max returned,
the booth was all dark.

Poor Maxie felt
a small lump in his throat.
Then tacked on the wall,
he saw a small note.

TO EXIT PETROPOLIS
PLEASE FOLLOW
THE SIGNS
NEXT TO THE POND
BY THE
CLUMP OF PINES.

But the signs by the pines
were not very nice,
having been chewed
by mischievous mice.

Would he ever get home?
His chances weren't great.
Max thought, scratched his nose,
then called out, "Wait!"

"That's it! I've got it!
Without a doubt,
I smelled my way in,
I'll smell my way out!"

With his nose to the ground,
he took big sniffs,
till he finally caught
the familiar whiffs . . .

. . . of Molly's wool sweater, Ted's shoes on the floor,

and followed that trail to the exit door. . . .

It wasn't so easy
to squeeze himself through.
(Too many pizzas
will do that to you.)

EXIT

The family was eager
at the end of their day
to see how Max fared
while they were away.

"Hey, Max!" Ted called.
"Did you use your new door?
You're right where we left you,
stretched out on the floor."

"Poor Maxie," sighed Molly,
"with nothing to do!"
Max smiled and rolled over.
If they only knew!

THE CITY of PETROPOLIS